# *Dear Parent:*
# *Your child's love of reading starts here!*

Every child learns to read in a different way and at his or her own speed. Some go back and forth between reading levels and read favorite books again and again. Others read through each level in order. You can help your young reader improve and become more confident by encouraging his or her own interests and abilities. From books your child reads with you to the first books he or she reads alone, there are I Can Read Books for every stage of reading:

### SHARED READING
Basic language, word repetition, and whimsical illustrations, ideal for sharing with your emergent reader

### BEGINNING READING
Short sentences, familiar words, and simple concepts for children eager to read on their own

### READING WITH HELP
Engaging stories, longer sentences, and language play for developing readers

### READING ALONE
Complex plots, challenging vocabulary, and high-interest topics for the independent reader

### ADVANCED READING
Short paragraphs, chapters, and exciting themes for the perfect bridge to chapter books

I Can Read Books have introduced children to the joy of reading since 1957. Featuring award-winning authors and illustrators and a fabulous cast of beloved characters, I Can Read Books set the standard for beginning readers.

A lifetime of discovery begins with the magical words "I Can Read!"

*Visit www.icanread.com for information*
*on enriching your child's reading experience.*

I Can Read!™

SHARED
My First
READING

# THE FALL FESTIVAL

## BY MERCER MAYER

HarperCollins*Publishers*

*To Tess, Tori, and Tedy Chapell*

I Can Read Book® is a trademark of HarperCollins Publishers.

Little Critter: The Fall Festival
Copyright © 2009 Mercer Mayer. All rights reserved. LITTLE CRITTER, MERCER MAYER'S LITTLE CRITTER and MERCER MAYER'S LITTLE CRITTER and logo are registered trademarks of Orchard House Licensing Company. All rights reserved.
Manufactured in the United States of America.
No part of this book may be used or reproduced in any manner whatsoever without written permission except in the case of brief quotations embodied in critical articles and reviews. For information address HarperCollins Children's Books, a division of HarperCollins Publishers, 10 East 53rd Street, New York, NY 10022.
www.icanread.com

Library of Congress catalog card number: 2008931803
ISBN 978-0-06-083552-1 (trade bdg.) —ISBN 978-0-06-083551-4 (pbk.)

Typography by Sean Boggs    13  14  15  16  LP/WOR  10 9 8 7   ❖    First Edition

A Big Tuna Trading Company, LLC/J. R. Sansevere Book
www.littlecritter.com

It is fall.

The leaves change colors.

They turn yellow and red.

We are driving in the car.

We drive to the Fall Festival.

Lots of critters are there.

We bring a wagon
to hold the things we buy.

I see so many apples.

I try one.

Mom pays the man.

Little Sister has apple cider.

She spills it.

It is sticky.

We go on a hayride.

There is not much hay.

We ride through
a field full of pumpkins.

I watch a critter
shoot pumpkins into the air.
They go SPLAT!

It is fun to watch.

We walk to the apple trees.

I see critters picking apples.

I get to pick apples, too.

Dad buys the apples that we pick.
Mom will make many apple pies.

Yum! I eat another apple.

Mom says, "No more apples."

Next we look for
a Halloween pumpkin.

Some pumpkins are too small.

Some pumpkins
are too funny looking.

I find the perfect pumpkin.
It is big.

Mom finds
the perfect pumpkin, too.
It is not so big.

We play the horseshoe game.

We each get three throws.

We can win prizes.

I go first.

I aim.

I throw.

I fly. Whoops!

I forgot to let go.

Dad goes next.

He wins every time.

He wins a bunny
for Little Sister
and a bear for me.

It is time to go home.

Little Sister pulls the wagon.

I help her.

Dad carries the pumpkin.
Mom picks up the apples
that we drop.

31

I think fall is great,

but I ate too many apples.